caillou ®

The Shopping Trip

Text: Nicole Nadeau • Illustrations: Claude Lapierre

chouette

"Caillou! We're going shopping,"
Mommy called. Caillou's baby sister
Rosie was all ready to go.
And Mommy had her coat on.

Mommy wanted to help Caillou
get dressed, but Caillou said,
"I want to do it myself."
He put on his coat.
Mommy helped him just a little
with the buttons.

Mommy put Rosie in her stroller.
"Caillou, do you want to help me push?"
Mommy asked.
Caillou didn't feel like pushing the stroller.
"I want to walk by myself," he replied.
He saw a nice stick and picked it up.
"Look, Mommy!"
Mommy admired Caillou's stick.

At the store, Caillou wanted to keep
his stick but he couldn't take it into the store.
"We could hide it," Mommy suggested.
"I want to do it myself,"
Caillou told her.
He hid his stick under a park bench.

Mommy put Rosie in the shopping cart.
Caillou didn't want to go in the cart.
He was too big for that.
He liked to walk down the aisles
by himself.

Caillou wandered away from
Mommy and Rosie.
He went shopping by himself.
Caillou stopped in front of some bags
of onions. He tried to pick one up,
but the bag was too heavy and
all the onions fell out.

Mommy came running, looking worried.
"Caillou, I've been looking
for you everywhere," she said.
Caillou hung his head in shame.
Mommy put the onions back on the shelf.

Mommy then put Caillou into
the shopping cart.
Mommy was annoyed. So was Caillou.
He didn't want to be in the store
any more.
He just wanted to go home.

Outside, Caillou sat in Rosie's stroller.
"Caillou, you're big enough to walk,"
Mommy told him.
"I'm too tired," Caillou complained.

"Don't forget your stick, Caillou,"
said Mommy.
Caillou ran to the bench.
His stick was still there. "My stick!"
shouted Caillou.

Caillou wasn't tired any more.
Now he felt like pushing his baby sister.
Caillou gave his stick to Mommy
and grabbed the handle of the stroller.
Caillou told Mommy proudly,
"I can do it myself."

We gratefully acknowledge the financial support of BPIDP, SODEC and the Canada Council for the Arts.

Text: Nicole Nadeau
Illustrations: Claude Lapierre

© 2001 Chouette Publishing

Canadian Cataloguing in Publication Data
Nadeau, Nicole, 1956-
Caillou, the shopping trip
(North star)
Translation of: Caillou, les courses.
For children aged 3 and up.

ISBN 2-89450-234-6

1. Shopping - Juvenile literature. I. Lapierre, Claude, 1942-   . II. Title.
III. Series: North star (Montreal, Quebec).

TX335.5.N32 2001   j640'.73   C00-941726-5

Printed in Canada
10 9 8 7 6 5 4